Hooray for Snail!
John Stadler

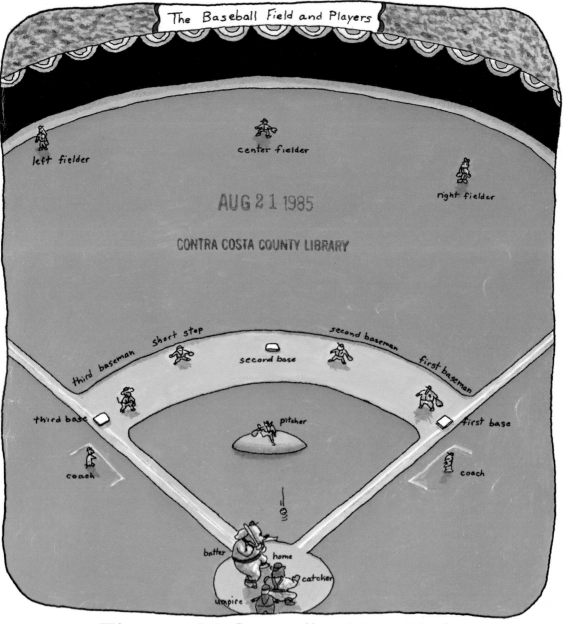

The Baseball Field and Players

left fielder

center fielder

right fielder

third baseman

short stop

second baseman

second base

first baseman

third base

first base

pitcher

coach

coach

batter

home

catcher

umpire

Thomas Y. Crowell   New York

Library of Congress Cataloging in Publication Data
Stadler, John.
    Hooray for snail!

    Summary: Slow Snail hits the ball so hard during
a baseball game that it flies to the moon and back.
Will Snail have time to slide in for a home run?
    [1. Snails—Fiction.   2. Baseball—Fiction]
I. Title.
PZ7.S77575Ho 1984   [E]   83-46164
ISBN 0-690-04412-7
ISBN 0-690-04413-5 (lib. bdg.)

To my teammates:

Bob Wesler

Rick Rennert

James Kanter

Bruce Longstreet

Snail is on the bench.

Snail listens.

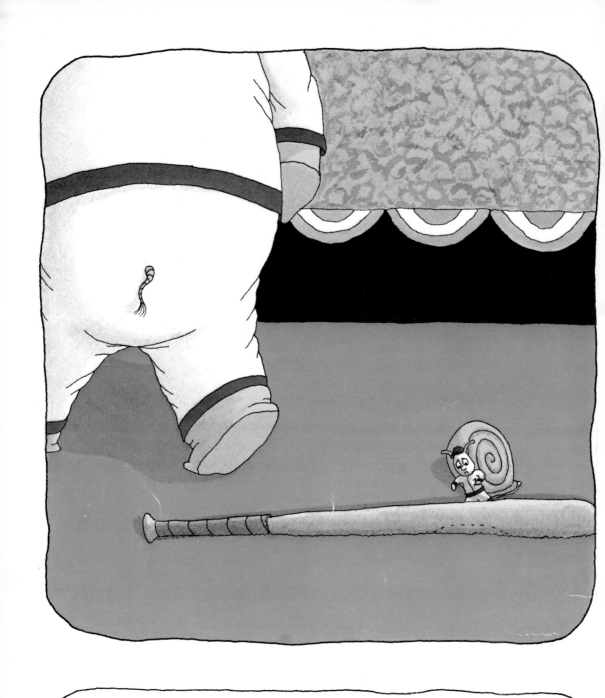

Snail gets the bat.

The bat is heavy.

Snail slams the ball.

The ball flies up.

Snail tips his hat.

The ball goes into space.

Hippo shouts.

Snail runs.

Snail is slow.

Snail is tired.

The ball hits the moon.

Snail is thirsty.

The ball starts back.

Snail is sleepy.

The ball bounces.

Snail races on.

The ball comes down.

The fielder sees the ball.

Snail runs faster.

The fielder throws the ball.

Here comes Snail.

Here comes the ball.

Snail slides home.

Boom!

Snail is out.

No. Snail is safe.

Snail wins the game.